Nat the Cat
Takes a Bath

By Jarrett Lerner

Ready-to-Read

Simon Spotlight

New York   London   Toronto   Sydney   New Delhi

For Soleia

SIMON SPOTLIGHT
An imprint of Simon & Schuster Children's Publishing Division
1230 Avenue of the Americas, New York, New York 10020
This Simon Spotlight edition May 2023
Copyright © 2023 by Jarrett Lerner
For information about special discounts for bulk purchases, please
contact Simon & Schuster Special Sales at 1-866-506-1949 or
business@simonandschuster.com.
Manufactured in the United States of America 0323 LAK
2 4 6 8 10 9 7 5 3 1
This book has been cataloged by the Library of Congress.
ISBN 978-1-6659-1894-7 (hc)
ISBN 978-1-6659-1893-0 (pbk)
ISBN 978-1-6659-1895-4 (ebook)

This is Nat.

Nat is a cat.

Nat the Cat
is going to
take a bath.

I said,
Nat the Cat
is going to
take a bath.

Why are you not
taking a bath,
Nat the Cat?

Nat the Cat,
are you scared
of the bath?

Oh!
You should have
said so.

One towel for Nat the Cat!

Okay, Nat the Cat.
NOW are you
going to
take a bath?

This is Pat.
Pat is a rat.

And I LOVE baths!